Read!

5 Silly Stories for Early Reader

A Little T-Rex Book

By Jeanne Schickli & Tara Cousins

Table of Contents

Book 1: Tom Cat

Book 2: Smiles & Frowns

Book 3: The King & His Ring

Book 4: That Ball

Book 5: The Twins & Silent E

Book 1:
Tom Cat

Tom Cat went on a walk.

1

Tom Cat went far.

2

He saw a frog.

3

He saw a car.

4

He saw a plane.

5

Tom Cat wanted milk.

Tom Cat went back.

7

He saw his home.

8

Tom Cat got his milk.

He is a glad cat.

Book 2:

Smiles & Frowns

I am a cowboy.

1

This is a smile.

This is a frown.

A smile is a frown upside down.

This is my smile.

This is my frown.

This is my smile upside down.

This is my frown upside down.

Now I am a clown with a frown.

9

Now I am a clown
with an upside
down frown.

Book 3:

The King & His

Ring

I am the king.

I know everything.

1

You are the king.

Do you know everything?

Then where is your ring?

I lost my ring!

3

I do not know everything.

Find my ring!

It rings.

8

This is your ring.

I am the king.

I know everything.

Book 4:

That Ball

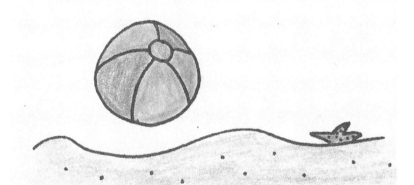

I toss the ball up.

Where is the ball?

2

The ball is on the tall wall.

The ball falls.

I get it.

4

I toss the ball way up.

Where will it go?

The ball is on the bell!

6

I pull the rope on the bell.

Ding dong!

The ball falls.

8

It went to the troll!

The troll wants a toll.

I give the troll a toll.

I get the ball!

·

Book 5:

The Twins &

Silent E

pin...pine

The pine feels like a pin.

cap...cape

We put a cap and a cape on the dog.

cub...cube

The cub ate the cube of ice.

car...care

Take care of Dad's car.

kit...kite

Is the box a kit for a kite?

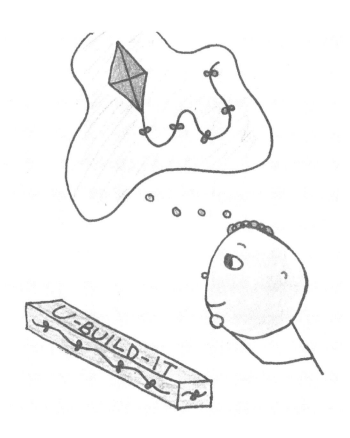

us...use

Use us to pull the wagon.

mad...made

Mom, do not be mad.
We made a cake.

hop...hope

I hope the rabbit can hop fast.

bit... bite

Let me take a bite.

Just a small bit.

not...note

Did you not get my note?

sam...same

Sam seems the same as Tom. Sam and Tom are twins.

The End

Thanks for reading!

Visit www.amazon.com for the other two books in the **Now I Can Read!** Series:

Volume 1: Short Vowel Sounds

Volume 2: Long Vowel Sounds

CPSIA information can be obtained
at www.ICGtesting.com
Printed in the USA
BVHW030210010322
630311BV00011B/57